Wandering Nights

Wandering Nights

Akin Fatimehin

AMVPS

Published by

AMV Publishing Services
259 Nassau Street Ste 2 #661
Princeton NJ 08542-4609
Tel: + 1 609-627-9168 - Fax: + 1 609-716-7224
emails: publisher@amvpublishingservices.com &
customerservice@amvpublishingservices.com
worldwide web: https://amvpublishingservices.com

Wandering Nights

This is a work of fiction. Names, characters, places, and incidents either are the product of the author's imagination or are used fictitiously. Any likeness or resemblance to actual persons, living or dead, events, or locales is entirely coincidental.

Copyright © 2022 Akin Fatimehin

All rights reserved. No part of this publication may be reproduced, stored in a retrieval system, or transmitted in any form or by any means, electronic, mechanical, photocopying, recording or otherwise without the written permission of the publisher.

Book & Cover Design: AMV Origination & Design Division

Library of Congress Control Number: 2021940505

ISBN: 978-978-965-338-6

Just Before the Nights

The heat of a typical West African afternoon must be the hottest thing next to the heat in hell. For this, kudos to the African who endures this scorching heat as he embarks on activities necessary for his subsistence. It is under this condition that an African street trader, with sweat caressing his brows, hawks his wares.

It is also under this infernal heat that the traffic warden regulates traffic. School children too are not left out of this onslaught, as they, with aching limbs, trod home from school under this scorching sun. Under the scorching sun, housewives also have their fair share as they scout for items with which to cook the day's meal for their children and husbands who busy themselves in various laboured tasks. Life a la typical West African afternoon is not easy. In fact, it could pass for hell. Real hell.

Not the nights. Night time in sub-equatorial Africa is a time for repose — repose for the soul as well as for the body. It is at night that the African stretches his cranking limbs and joints. Night is when the feeling of love and bliss prevails in his mind. Night is when he gets drunk on his beer, palm wine or *ogogoro*, and staggers home drunkenly, singing in unbalanced tones. On reaching home, he makes passionate love to his wife.

Friend, I tell you, night in Africa, West of the sahara, is a time for love and friendship.

Love and friendship. Those are the two things I sought on those nights when I combed the entire city. The other things I sought were knowledge and understanding. But, maybe, ought to pause here and give you an idea of who I am. Sorry, who I was.

This guy who now communicates with you was a fresh product of the National Youth Service Corps scheme or sham. Subsequent to that, he had graduated in Philosophy and Political Science from one of the universities in the land. I talk about myself as if I was talking about somebody else because we — "That Guy" and I — are basically two different people. How? Well, That Guy is naive and inexperienced while I am more experienced and knowledgeable; thanks to those nights.

Am I getting ahead of myself in this story? Am I mixing things up a wee bit?

I had graduated from university. I had completed National Youth Service, still I did not know what purpose those two experiences served in my life. Of what relevance were the Kantian Theories and Foreign Policy Studies to the everyday needs of my country? To what extent could I apply Plato's dialogues and African resistance to western imperialism to the things which affected my countrymen most - hunger, disease, poverty, inequality and disunity?

The National Youth Service sham, for indeed that was what it was, had only further accentuated my confusion. As far as I was concerned, it was an introduction into the delights of alcohol, tobacco and sex for erstwhile teetotallers and near virgins. The scheme was a shadow coating for the unemployment problem in the country. Imagine one year; a bloody whole year wasted on drinking and wanton promiscuity, at the end of which you could not utter a mono syllable of the language spoken in the area where you served. In most cases, you couldn't marry a girl from that area because they were only good bedmates. Also, it was either the area itself was too waterlogged, too humid, or infested with too many flies? Who would want to spend the rest of his life in a place like that? Home was much better. Home sweet home....

However, quite a number of corpers were prepared to remain in their areas of posting. I guess they were those who were more concerned with the unity of the country. The guys were willing to marry the native girls, rear kids, and settle down to work. But then, getting a job had its challenges. Who would give work to a "stranger" when there were thousands of "sons of the soil" in the labour market? Thousands of indigenes who were not, well.... so qualified, but at least they were indigenes.

These and other thoughts swirled in my head when I was let loose. That was simply what it was — being let loose. Like being demobilized after a war in the jungle, complete with full military parade uniforms, pips, swords bugle and all.

You were given a piece of paper which they called a discharge certificate which you didn't fully understand.

What could you do? In the mornings you woke up and combed the entire city. From establishment to establishment, you went, donning a T-shirt tucked neatly into a pair of jeans trousers on canvas shoes, and looking immaculate. Brandishing your 2'1 and the piece of paper called a discharge certificate given to you, you never gave up. After all, this was your country where you had to stay and salvage. But what you were trying to salvage was seeking to destroy you, or how else would you explain the fact that just the other day, you saw Frank driving past. Frank of course was your classmate. The class dullard, whom the lecturers had done a big favour by letting off with a mere pass.

He parked when he saw you and both of you got talking. Of course, the car was his, and so were the pin-striped suit and silk tie he had on, including the crocodile skin shoes. And of course, he had a job. Something-something executive in something-something company. The same company where the personnel manager had painstakingly explained to you why, although they really needed you, they couldn't offer you employment because of the major shares government had in the company. Of course you knew. You also knew that Frank's uncle was a commissioner in government. This country belongs to us all; indeed.

That was when I began my night combing. Booze was supposed to shut my eyes to reality. The golden fluid, they said, worked wonders with a guy's psyche. And I needed answers. Those to provide those answers were the intellectuals. Not the ivory tower dons who bombarded you with ideological balderdash and intellectual garbage, but the genuine intellectuals. The whores, the rogues, the unemployed, the barmen, the common people whose daily experiences and life had bestowed with genuine intellect. Those were the people I met on my night wanderings, and they it was who provided long sought answers to long asked questions. The answers came in the form of dialogues, overhead soliloquies and stories which I heard.

Friend, why not follow as I relate to you a few of these stories. Maybe if you pay sufficient attention to them there could be something to be learnt. Maybe. Just maybe.

Polly's Tale

I met Polly at a bar named *Wazobia*. True to it's name, Wazobia's clientele reflected people from all walks of life and the four corners of the nation. There was no discrimination whatsoever when it came to clients at Wazobia.

All and sundry — from the highest executive to the lowliest labourer — came to Wazobia for a good time. It was an edifice built with bamboo bars. The hardwood carvings, thatched roof and dim lights further gave it an exotic African look. At full capacity, Wazobia could contain three hundred guests. Outside was a vast expanse of land on which night fires were usually lit for the sole purpose of roasting bush meat. The drinks varied as much as the patrons. There was palm wine, beer, stout, local gin and all manner of imported spirits. The kitchen's speciality was it's pepper soup — a dark, foul-looking concoction, sprinkled with exotic leaves and containing all manner of cooked animal carcass, ranging from beef, to cow liver, to tripe, to goat's penis. It's taste belied it's look. The pepper drew tears from your eyes and mucus from your nose. The meat was tastier than tasty. All in all, that stew was the best thing man had ever cooked for man. And it sold for a naira.

And then the girls? They came in all shapes and sizes — big buttocked, average buttocked, small buttocked, massive, average, small breasted with nipples threatening to burst through see through blouses; waists swaying and buttocks swinging.

There was music which blared softly from the six hundred watt loud speakers.

The girls brought delight and joy to the lives of the men who came to Wazobia.

The first hint I heard as regards the existence of Polly drew from a remark passed by one of the girls. She was tall and dark with hair plaited in true African fashion. Her breasts were average and stood at right angles. Her long straight legs which flared slightly at the hips seemed to melt into a waist that looked as though it were designed to fit into a man's palm. When she walked she seemed to float. Floating was her mode of locomotion. When she floated it was as if she was walking. She once floated beside where I was sitting and I couldn't help exclaiming loudly "Whao".

"What was that?" asked the gentleman whose table I shared.

"Did you see the girl who just walked by?" I said, gesturing so he could see who I meant.

"Sure," he nodded. "I've had her, she isn't as good as Polly. Polly is the best, man," he concluded as he downed his beer and left, leaving me to ponder over the mysterious Polly.

Any girl who was "better" — I wasn't too sure what that meant — than the angel I had just seen had to be truly ultimate. And indeed she was.

She came a week after the night of my comment on the other girl. She walked into Wasobia and every head turned. And by that I mean to the last head. Six hundred optical zones stared at her as if magnetized.

Polly was a half caste. She glowed like only naturally light-complexioned people did. The truth about Polly was that if you put her alone in a room, she would stand out. With a hundred, she would still stand out. A thousand, a million, a billion, a goddamn fucking zillion and you still had her illuminating the entire horizon.

Another truth about her was that she was a whore. But you wouldn't know except someone told you or she told you herself. Which she did. But I'll come back to that. On that night, she was wearing a green dress which sort of accentuated her curves. What in God's name am I talking about? Nothing could accentuate Polly's curves. They were an accentuation in their own right. As she stood at the entrance of Wazobia, it seemed as if time stood still. For those twenty seconds or so, it was like all hearts had stopped beating, like all clocks and watches had stopped ticking.

Polly caught the cue and stood still for those momentary seconds. Then when it seemed as if the spell was wearing out, as if hearts had again began to beat and clocks began to tick, she started to pace; no, to stride; no.... It would amount to a waste of time to attempt to describe the way Polly walked or indeed anything about her. Only a surrealist could. Even his own account would not be complete.

I could not take my eyes off her. As she walked or glided or swam or whatever one chose to call her mode of locomotion, I followed her with my eyes and then for a second, our eyes met, I saw it all there. Recognition, even though I had never before met her in my life. Love, though I didn't know what it meant; passion, even if it was killing me. I felt like a little boy from the village being introduced to the delights of Tinubu Square.

Just before she took her eyes away from me, I thought, honestly thought, I saw a smile. When she looked away, sadness engulfed me. For I knew that much as I desired I could never have her. True, at this time I had not known she was a whore but even if I knew, it couldn't have helped matters. For her price would be too high for me. Out of reach for an unemployed ex-corper who depended on handouts from his parents. Still, if Polly told me she needed anything, I would have gotten it. If she wanted a star, I would have spent my entire life building a rocket with which to fetch her one. If she needed a mountain, I could have brought it to her.

A gentle tap on my shoulder brought me out of my reverie. The person who had tapped me whispered something into my ear and all else became a blur.

I found myself walking behind the most beautiful girl who had ever inhabited planet earth. Through the haze I saw male eyes regarding me with jealousy and envy. Then we were outside. Out in the open, I heard the most beautiful voice.

"You want to have yourself a trip?"

"I.... I don't understand," I stammered.

"You want me?" I again heard. Now my head was beginning to clear.

"Yes, but...." I lost my voice.

"Normally, you would have to pay. But I'm giving it to you for free. You probably can't afford it anyway but I like you. I like you a lot. I loved the far away look that was on your face when you were seated inside."

Now it was clear to me. The possessor of the heavenly physiognomy which I was intently staring into was offering herself to me for free. And there I was stammering. I, the master seducer of virgins in the riverine area where I had done my youth service was stammering like an idiot at the offer of the most divine body that had ever offered itself to my optics. Then I allowed instinct to take over. She was in my arms and I was kissing her. The wettest, softest kiss a guy ever gave or took. We trodded arm in arm towards the iroko tree which was rumoured to be the domicile of a vast majority of night spirits behind Wazobia. There it was I had her with the moon and stars, and probably the spirits as the only spectators. Her moans and sighs mingled with my own oohs and aahs which in turn combined with the shrieks and hisses of a thousand night insects to produce an eerie ecstatic din. When it was over, I fumbled in my pockets for a cigarette, my angel also requested for one. Lighting up, I noticed that my angel's cheeks were wet. She had been sobbing quietly. This I couldn't understand. For I couldn't imagine Polly in tears, when, without even uttering a single word, she could have the whole world on her side. It was inconceivable.

Like a politician bursting into tears after rending his most earth-shattering speech on the soap box, that was what I thought but then I was only being stupid. Everybody cried. Even the stone-hearted, cold-blooded men cried. How could I expect Polly to be an exception. Still I couldn't understand what the source of her tears were. This I asked her. First, I thought she wasn't going to answer. The silence lingered on for a while as I figured what to say next when I heard her.

"It's nothing really, it's just that sometimes I feel sad about the way the whole world has turned out."

Ii must be her conscience, I thought. Someone once said whores (professionals and amateurs) always felt bad if and when they find someone they truly love. Which was why I sought to console her.

"Don't think too much about it," I said. "Sometimes, it is better to forget the past."

"But how can I? she asked. My entire present and future rests upon that past; I can't forget it. The injustice it entails is too much to permit my forgetting it."

That had me irked. I believe there is a perverse urge in all human beings which makes them want to listen to other people's miseries. Mine was fully aroused.

"Want to talk about it love?" I asked. "Get it off your chest," I added.

"Sure," she said, sitting up and allowing her naked breasts to swing provocatively. She pulled a last drag from her cigarette, threw the butt away and exhaled the smoke through her nostrils and then began to tell me what I had earlier referred to as Polly's Tale.

*****

"I was born twenty six years ago, the product of a British father, Joseph Guldard and a Calabar woman whose maiden name was Mary Ekpo. I was christened Paulina Guldard, but cannot remember being called that name. People — and that means everybody — had always called me Polly. Being the last of my parent's children, I had four elder brothers — Nathaniel, David, Lawrence, and Albert. We had a splendid childhood; I was our father's pet, but that is an understatement. I was everybody's pet. I never saw or met anybody who did not like me or who tried to hurt me. With this feeling of being liked by everybody, I developed an attitude that later served to my detriment.

"I couldn't bear to hurt anybody — physically or psychologically. A friend, dressed in near rags could ask me how her dress looked, and rather than tell her the truth, I would tell her it was the most exquisite piece of clothing I had ever seen. One of my brothers would break one of my father's prized hardwares and knowing fully well that he would receive the beating of his life for that folly, I would volunteer that I broke it, knowing that my father would never lift a finger on me. I had that effect on people.

"One of the people who so loved me was my class teacher. At every point in time, he never ceased to show his affection for me. One day, he invited me to his apartment, and I obliged. As I sat on his bed, he began to murmur incoherently. Among what I could decipher from his blabbing was that he loved me. That was all I needed to hear. I seated him on his bed and cradled his head in my arms. I felt like a mother, his mother. I noticed that his sobs had subsided. I began to enjoy my role.

"I told him I loved him too. When he heard that, he stopped sobbing completely, too fast. He began to fondle me. At first, I thought he was only trying to repay me for the comfort I had offered him. But then he began to kiss me, I wanted protest but I couldn't; I mean, the part of my body which was supposed to do the protesting was the one being kissed and by the time that orifice was set free, I no longer felt like protesting because by then, I had began to enjoy his caresses. Gently, he undressed me and by the time he began to remove my under things, I no longer had a care in the world. Thus began my career at ardour. Having so much enjoyed it and perceiving that my teacher would come by some harm if I told anyone, and not wanting to hurt him as I never wanted to hurt anybody, I kept my mouth shut.

"Being my naive self, I still believed nothing would go wrong. When after the first month, my period which I was just growing accustomed to failed to show up, I just thought it was a normal thing. Nobody had schooled me about things like that; nobody imagined I could be indiscreet."

"So, at the second and third months, I began to show visible signs of something strange about me. I was spitting and vomiting incessantly; nobody, least of all me, thought anything was wrong. But then at the fourth month, by which time my stomach had protruded slightly, my mother noticed. I told her the truth, and surprisingly she didn't ask who I did it with. She waited for my father before taking any decision. It was he who made the fuss.

The first thing he did was to ask me who did it. Then he stormed my school and threatened to kill the teacher. I mean, he would have committed murder had the poor teacher been around. Fortunately, he wasn't and with much persuasion, my father was pacified. When he came back home, he, my mother and I held a small conference. The topic was sex education. They blamed themselves for what happened and vowed never to let it happen again.

"The next day, they took me to a doctor who gave me a sedative and I fell asleep instantly. When I woke up, my mother was there and the doctor said I could go home. After that, nobody ever talked about any pregnancy at home. School was a different thing. Although no one spoke about it openly, it was there. In the way people talked and looked at me, I had acquired the unspoken reputation of being the school whore. The teacher went away but that didn't make matters any better. I lost concentration. I began to feel like a recluse. I isolated myself. The few friends I had, began to avoid me. It was a down period in my life, the lowest anyone could go. The immediate consequence was that I failed my final examinations woefully and that was the end of my educational career. For I was one person who intensely hated failing in any endeavour I set for myself. I like to be the best in all I do which is probably why I'm a damned good whore. Anyway I had a talk with my parents and they asked me the next step I wanted to take. Being very much in love with animals, I elected to work on one of my father's many farms. It was an occupation which I believed I had an affinity for.

"About this time, my four brothers were also making up their minds on various careers. Nathaniel, the eldest decided to be a priest. He went to the seminary and everybody was proud of him. David chose to become a doctor and was already in the university studying Medicine. Lawrence hoped to become a lawyer, and like David, was studying Law at the university, while Albert, the youngest of the four, was in higher school. He had set a goal for himself of becoming a member of the fourth estate of the realm. Things again began to go well. Happiness and love reigned supreme in our household. One day, what I had dreaded most in my life happened. My father went away and never came back. But not in the way it had been rumoured that he would. He suffered a heart attack in the dead of night and never survived it. Our entire household was thrown into disarray. My mother went into total panic. Nathaniel, my elder brother who had become a full fledged priest by this time was the rallying force. He gathered his wits together and took total control of the situation. His precision was something to marvel at and he always remained calm.

We buried our father but my mother was never the same again. The shock was too much for her. She could not imagine life without her beloved husband. I think it was this shock that took her life. She slept one night and never woke up. Thus the Guldard brothers and sister became orphans. Nathaniel became the head of the household. Again, we all marvelled at the "ruthless" precision with which he dealt with varying situations. We were all proud of him. After the effects of our parents death had worn off, it was time to read my father's will. That revealed a lot of thoughtfulness on my father's part. At least, I thought so. We were to sell all his property except one farmland which I was to continue managing. The proceeds from the sales were to be used for the following purposes:

1) To build Nathaniel a cathedral which would be the largest in the land.
2) For David to set up the largest medical practice in the land.
3) For Lawrence to do the same in the legal field.
4) For Albert to establish a newspaper in the land.

"We did all these to the last letter and everybody went their separate ways. Still we remained a very close knit family. We saw each other frequently and exchanged letters and telegrams a great deal. Then Nathaniel began to develop a strange behaviour. Envy. His calling did not permit him to marry. So while his brothers were getting married, he remained single and celibate. At least that was what we thought.

"But rather than direct his envy and jealously towards it's immediate source, he chose me to pour out his pent up frustration. At first he didn't attack me directly; he shrouded his envy in the form of pontification. It was a sin for a young woman to change lovers like she changed underclothes, he always admonished. It was evident that he was referring to me, since at that time I had not tied the nuptial cord, though I had plenty of suitors. Still I chose to bid my time. I tried to make sure that when I finally did take the plunge, the choice I made would be the right one. Yet I was not averse to little physical pleasures. I had grown to understand the type of pleasure which my body gave to men and the amount it equally received from the same. I made no pretence and I had no apologies to the effect that I enjoyed sex. This, my brother called "whoring around", and that I would rot in eternal hell fire.

"The other level on which my envious brother "attacked" me was that of finance. It was glaring to all that my farm was doing better than his church. This made me far wealthier than he was. He would accuse me of being in love with worldly things and not sharing the proceeds with my workers equally. When I tried to do this, he would complain that I was over pampering them, wanting them to be like me.

"At this stage, my other brothers tried to come to my rescue. Lawrence, the lawyer was the most vocal. He would come out in outright terms and tell Nathaniel to mind his business. My life and land were mine to do as I wished. He urged Nathaniel to stay in his cathedral and put his own house in order first before trying to tell others what to do. The rumour going around was that Nathaniel's church was in disarray. Word went round that dissent reigned supreme among his assistants and lieutenants. We never knew how true or false this rumour was.

"Despite all his shortcomings, Nathaniel always knew how to put up a face. No matter the intensity of the chaos, Nathaniel always remained calm. When questioned about the dissent in his church, he would contort his face in a stern look, stand up ramrod straight and bellow out in his deep baritone voice: "We are all together", and everyone would believe him. Whether this belief arose out of genuine thoughts of the truthfulness of his words, or out of fear for him, I would not know. Still, we all believed him. And that was all that mattered.

"Then came a time when there was a minor uprising on my farm. I think it had something to so with selection of birds for sale. There was an argument as to whether we should sell the broilers or the layers.

"Some of my assistants opined that we should sell the broilers and allow the layers to remain since the layers could always breed other broilers. But the other camp believed we should sell the layers, since broiler meat was prime food, and we stood to gain a lot. As a result of fighting between the two camps, the poultry house, as well as a few houses of key members of the opposing camp, were burnt down. In the evening when it become evident that I could no longer contain the situation, I sent for Lawrence, who having appraised the situation and finding nothing he could do about it, called Nathaniel.

Nathaniel came with his assistants. The first thing they did was quell the chaos. This made me happy a great deal. But my joy was short-lived as the next thing he did was invite me for a chat in my office.

'It is now glaring that you are not capable of holding the exalted office which has been bestowed upon you. I am therefore expelling you from it with immediate effect. You have a choice. Either you stay on this farm and work for your keep like everyone else or you leave it forever, as I am taking its management for a yapping session.'

"I was incensed. I tried to fight him in all the ways I knew and with all the weapons I had, but it was glaring even to me that I couldn't win because first, he was the custodian and executor of our father's will, and had therefore adjusted the will to fit his every whim and caprice. Second, he had this long and weird looking staff he and his assistants carried around. Rumour had it that the staff had supernatural powers, and that anyone it was pointed at was doomed forever. It was that staff, which I feared more than anything else. My brothers could also not help. I guess they too were scared shit of the staff. Either that or they too were scared of not forfeiting the crumbs Nathaniel was passing down to them.

"On one or two occasions, Albert who owned a media house, tried to stand up to him. On each of these occasions, Nathaniel always had him locked up in a dungeon at the back of the farm house which was reserved for animals that had gone gaga. After those inhuman experiences, Albert was all praises for Nathaniel. Lawrence in his own case had always been greedy. His loyalties always stood where he knew he could reap the greatest benefits. I later learnt that he had been my staunch supporter only because of the chickens and turkeys I sent to him every Christmas. Now that those Yuletide animals were no longer forthcoming, he knew where to place his allegiance. It was rumoured that he did not have enough facilities with which to fight his humanitarian battle. This was his one problem which seemed to be the only thing he bothered about.

"Thus, it was that I began to peddle my ass for bread. I, however, made up my mind that if I was going to become a whore, I was going to be the damned best. You can see, I'm not doing badly. My clientele are the best of the best and they pay well too. Men don't derive satisfaction from their wives any longer and are willing to pay exquisite money for an exquisite substitute. Along the way, I have even received a few proposals of marriage but each time, I have refused. I don't think I can ever make a good wife to a man.

"Ha, before I forget, there was one occasion when Nathaniel called me back to manage the farm. He said he had pressing problems to attend to at the cathedral.

"I jumped at the opportunity. After all, the farm was my rightful possession. But on reaching there, I was saddened by what I saw. All my former assistants had become corrupt. They had all developed rosy cheeks and had bought big cars and houses. Nothing was right again in my beloved farm. I tried my best. God knows I tried but the entire system had already been bedevilled by rot. The only way one could save that edifice was to wipe out the entire population, and of course that was impossible. Even the animals were corrupt, spoilt and pampered. In the end, I had no option than to join in the indecency. That was the only excuse my brother, Nathaniel, needed. He came back, brandishing hell and outrage. He threw me out and declared, 'It seems as if you have learnt no lesson from history.'

"He thus looked over the place again. But things weren't as good as he said he'd make them. The dissent in his cathedral had already made in roads into the farm. Corruption remained at its highest. Farm implements were daily deteriorating; farm animals were hardly well fed. There was chaos everywhere.

"Nathaniel is in no way better than me. He is a bully," Polly said, concluding her story.

I leave the judgment for you, dear reader.

The Barman's Tale

I went to Wazobia on the next night but Polly was nowhere to be found. And then the next. I did not bother to ask about her. Nobody, I was sure, would know of her whereabouts. One thing I had though been able to deduce from her discourse was that she was a wanderer. She would find another John whom she would shack up with for two to three weeks, and when she realized that fellow was falling in love with her, she would zap!

As you probably might have deduced from her tale, Polly is no longer capable of going along with a deep mutual emotional attachment. A few people with whom I have discussed her with attribute this to her humaneness. After all, she is human. Once again, the final judgment is yours to make.

After about a week of no Polly, I stopped visiting Wazobia, for the place had turned out for me a night firmament with no stars. Wazobia without Polly was for me a barren desert.

But severing ties with Wazobia did not imply that I was severing ties with my quest for knowledge. Where else could one obtain knowledge, save for those night zones where a thousand neurological anatomies consciously or sub-consciously vocalized their thoughts?

The next place I visited was a hotel named *Three Three Three*. When I first paid the place a visit, I could not understand the name. But what tuned me into a regular customer was the Bartender. On your first visit to the place, he would ask you what you would drink. Within a split second of your reply, he was back and pouring the drink into a tumbler. After that, he never bothered to ask you anything else.

Orisagbemi, the Barman, knew every customer by name. Some people whose specialty was to consume mixed spirits said of Orisagbemi, that he could mix any drink and the concoction would still taste right. He was always innovating and experimenting with drinks. Rumour had it that He had once mixed Cofta cough syrup with Nivaquine syrup. The "product", they said, tasted jovial. Many amiable gentlemen regularly thronged Three Three Three, who made my nights memorable.

Rumour had it that Orisagbemi was an incurable alcoholic and drug addict. That these were responsible for his perpetually being "high" and gaiety, and why he was always joking, laughing and smiling. His cool exterior was a shadow masking of the inner turmoil borne out of certain injustices which had been heaped upon him earlier in life.

Orisagbemi, the Barman was, in short, an unhappy man. That was what they said. And who wouldn't be unhappy to be in the bar, and in the same hotel that had his father-in-law as managing director and his wife as general manager? But how could one be sure? How was one to believe that the pot-bellied short man in his early fifties, who was always smoking cigars, was kith and kin, albeit through marriage, with Orisagbemi?

How could one believed that the light complexioned lady who daily dressed up in the most exquisite dresses and jewels, and whose immaculate shoes made clinking sounds when she walked, was Orisagbemi's wife?

Many questions! Who could one ask? There was no way, absolutely no way, except one chose to ask one of the three principal actors. And which better choice was there than Orisagbemi himself?

The opportunity offered itself on a cold rainy night. I guess the rain had kept a vast majority of the customers at home, and the few who came hastily downed their drinks and presumably returned to the comfort provided by the warmth of their homes. As midnight approached, the only two people left at the bar were the bartender and the night wanderer. Just as I was debating whether to have one more bottle or leave for my domicile. Orisagbemi appeared from behind his bar and placed a bottle in front of me.

"This one is on the house," he said, setting himself on the chair opposite mine. He had also brought along a beer for himself and soon we started chatting.

At first our conversation was measured — two strangers sizing each other up. But soon the alcohol began to take its toll, and loosened our tongues, and we began to grow unwary of each other. I told him about my futile search for a job; about my family and how they were pressuring me to go back to school to learn more of the rubbish which I was trying to purge myself off of. I told him a lot but he told me a lot more. I did not need to ask him. He opened up his soul to me as though he had known me for ages. He told me the story about his life, the sum total of his experiences, past and present. It is that story that I now relate to you.

****

He was born into a poor home, a very poor one. His father was a peasant farmer while his mother traded in petty goods. Living under these harsh conditions, 'Gbemi (as he was mostly called), right from the time he could grasp the essence of meaning, realized that the only way he could make something out of life was to get an education. Thus he totally devoted himself to his studies in the non-fee paying elementary school which he attended. He was not by any means a brilliant student, but he was a dogged one; a determined one. He would spend hours pondering over anything his teachers taught that was not clear to him. Although he never came first, second or third, he never came last, second to last or third to last either. He was always conveniently at the middle of the pack.

Then came the time to proceed to secondary school. And that would have proved a dead end due to his parent's meagre earnings. There was absolutely no way this dream could come true, but this young lad was obsessed with the idea of educating himself.

He soon came up with a solution. This solution, however, would sever ties with his parent's religious belief. His parents were practicing and devout idol worshippers.

'Gbemi knew that if he was going to get secondary education, it could only be through a Christian missionary scholarship. To obtain this, he knew he had to denounce his parent's religious beliefs, and sever completely the ties which bound him to *Ifa*, the deity which his parents worshipped. He would lose his birth identity forever. But he reasoned that all this was a small price to pay for secondary education, and knew that this would not be easy. For him being an only child, he realized his parents would not accede easily. He thus set for himself the task of systematically convincing them. During conversations with his father, he would mention the names of great citizens and of the kind of lives they lived. Automobiles, fancy clothes, big houses, big offices and of course plenty of money.

"Wouldn't you be proud to have a son who was the possessor of all these?" he always questioned his father.

With this systematic approach, 'Gbemi had no problem receiving approval from his parents when the time came for him to start secondary school.

It was the norm then for beneficiaries to be handed over to the care of the village pastor or Bishop. 'Gbemi was no exception, he became a ward to the village pastor, Bishop Alaba Berkley. The first thing the old reverend gentleman made him do was to adopt a Christian name, and changed his name to Christopher. Christopher became one of the church vergers and a member of the church choir. His sweet sounding voice and neat appearance turned him into some kind of favourite with the church elders. At school, Christopher was also a very diligent chap. He never missed classes, never argued with his teachers and outshone all in sports. He was loved by all and sundry.

The church had taught him as a youth the tenets of obedience, and that as a Christian, he had to love his fellow men as himself. e was admonished to obey the Ten Commandments, and abstain from earthly pleasures and that the moral end to be sought in all he did was the will of God. The church had all the answers. Well, almost all the answers, for as Christopher progressed in years, he began to see contradictions between what the church preached and what obtained in life. For one, men did not love others as they did themselves. At least, he Christopher did not. It wasn't that he did not try. It was just that it seemed impracticable. Maybe unnatural was the word. It was unnatural for anybody to love someone else the way they loved themselves. Christopher began to train himself in the art of reasoning, trying to critically analyses situation and to deduce concrete solutions. But this solution was far from coming. How, for instance, was one going to explain that the church which preached obedience had the pastors and elders always at each other's necks.

The age-long rancour, a hard nut which proved tough for Christopher to crack, was the logic behind the church which prayed all to shun wealth and all earthly pleasures, and prayed for members of its congregation to attain wealth. The two did not cohere, Christopher reasoned. For instance, there were services for special prayers. There was a businessman who was never lucky in business. Every enterprise he tried his hands on always ended up crumbling. Christopher, on a few occasions overheard the pastors' prayers for this man:

"Father, may your son's business thrive. May he reap where he has sown. Pour your heavenly mercies on him...."

Christopher had a special interest in this man. His interest was aroused principally because rumour had it that the man was a widower. That his wife had died giving birth to his only child — a daughter who was about Christopher's age. This was the major reason for Christopher's interest in the man because lately, he had been having dreams about the girl. Not the ordinary Christian schoolboy dreams, but passionate, love-infected dreams from which he would wake up to discover a sticky wetness between his legs.

This was the third axe Christopher had to grind with God or the church or whoever was in control of such things. For how could those dreams which was the best thing that had happened to him in long time constitute a sin? And that was what the church preached. That things which brought pleasure to the body, whether thought about, dreamt or acted out, were sins. Christopher pondered over this for a long time and finally came up with an answer which he thought explained everything. The church was wrong. On that one issue, the church had misinterpreted God. For if God thought it was a sin, he would never allow it to happen. And wasn't it God who was responsible for what a men dreamt about? It couldn't be wrong.

Christopher's thoughts did not stop at the dreams. Even the act could not be bad. Wasn't it in the scriptures? Solomon and his concubines. With that resolution, his mind came to a rest. He knew in his heart of hearts that when the time came, he would know the right thing to do. It came sooner than he expected.

As a verger in the fourth form, he came across a young woman of about 35 years, and a member of his church. Vergers were usually designated to help the elderly and widows with household chores after service on Sundays. As fate would have it, he was designated to help this woman. Things went on without any incident of particular note for about three months. He would cut the grass, wash dishes or clothes and then leave. Then the woman began to prepare lunch for him. She then resorted to giving him presents — a shilling here, a shilling there. And then the queer looks; kind of undressing him mentally. Then one day she seduced him and initiated him into the delights of lovemaking. After that, there was no stopping him. He would have quickies with choir girls and *wham-bang-thank-you-ma'am* with frustrated wives of members of the laity. Soon he began to acquire the reputation as the church stud. Still he was not satisfied.

The real object of his desire was the businessman's daughter. She, he was sure, was the woman God had created for him, and until he had her, he knew his mind would not rest. Yet, it was not easy. For whenever he saw her, she was with her father. Their relationship was bounded on his incestuous. He never let her out of his sight and neither she him. If only she would join the choir. That was the only way. But it didn't happen. Then one day, when he was in his fifth form. He saw her alone for the first time. She had come to his guardian, the pastor's home, with a message from her father. As she was about to leave, he slipped her a note on which he had written in his boyish scrawl:

> *I love you, you are the Eve and I am the Adam, you are the sugar in my tea, the only mosquito in my net.*

That was all he needed. He didn't know her name and didn't want to know. As far as he was concerned, they had become lovers. When, during the next service he caught her smiling coyly at him, he ceased comprehending what the preacher was preaching about. He was smitten, madly in love. Then as if providence was in concert with him, the girl, Oluronke, joined the choir.

Theirs was the most secret affair there ever was. But that did not overshadow the effect it had. They were the two happiest youths in the whole of the district. Soon he was teaching her tunes on the piano and they began to have more time to themselves alone and it was bound to happen. All love relationships inevitably graduates into the physical. At first it was a kiss on the cheek, then on the lips — full and wet, with saliva transporting from one month to the other. Then touching of breasts. A sigh. A moan. Then the real act. And the deed was done. Love consummated. But what lover and loved failed to realize was that one deed had blended spermatozoa with ova.

For those who do not know, an embryonic foetus is the product of such union. A month, two and the discovery is made. Yes, by daddy, the businessman who comes storming into church with the good news. Shock. The waves are spent rippling through the length and breath of the church. Our hero is expelled. Along with his expulsion goes his church scholarship.

Back home, head bowed and tail between legs. And all thinks the matter is closed. But, providence is again watching. Ronke's father still far from attaining his business ambitions insists that Christopher must marry his daughter. He would not have a bastard grandchild, he echoes. And so at the age of eighteen, our hero gets married and moves into the abode of his father in-law.

The matrimonial relationship matured into a business one. Christopher became the personal assistant to Ronke's father and it was no coincidence that the rise in Ronke's father's business fortunes came at about this time. Christopher exhibited much business brilliance and industry. His organizational capabilities surpassed those that were expected of anybody of his age. Soon he had carved a niche for himself in the business world. Yet, he remained to be satisfied. What he worked for was not his. All he received in the form of remuneration was by all standards, considering the volume of work he did, paltry. He was still obsessed with the idea of rising to a very prominent position in the world. Where he had earlier believed that education was the key to that ascent, he now thought business was it. The kind of business he was involved in, his father- in- law's, was that of middleman. They would procure goods — a wide variety of them — from manufacturers, and then resell to retailers. Christopher realized that the profit made by his father-in-law was such that could permit another middleman. Thus, he resigned from his father-in-law's establishment and went about the process of acquiring funds like a man possessed. There was nothing he didn't do. No job did he consider to be beneath him. He drove cabs, dug trenches, washed dishes. At the end, he made his money, as a middleman. In no time, he was rich, but not as rich as he would have wanted to be, but at least he was comfortable. He and his wife moved out of his father-in-law's abode and had their second kid. He bought a car and was able to set up for his wife a lucrative business. Still, he was not satisfied. Christopher knew he had the doggedness and capability to get to the top, the very top. He would not stop until he achieved his aim, he resolved. For a long time, he had his eyes on the hotel business.

He knew that through dint of hard work, the sky was the limit. He began to conceive the plan in his mind, of an hotel which would be the ultimate, which would cater for almost everybody's taste — oriental, continental and foreign. A hotel which would accommodate everybody, both the rich and the poor. He got hold of every piece of literature he could on hostelling and catering.

What he had in mind was beyond the reach of the resources he had in hand. If he was to attain his desired goal, he needed partners. These he decided to seek.

Naturally, the first person he went to was his father-in-law; the man who had given him his first break in business. He had 30% of the initial capital, he explained to the old man. If he was willing to part with another 30%, he would find investors to cough out the other 40%. The old man readily acceded. He had grown to respect every business move his young son-in-law initiated.

Christopher was besides himself with joy. The 40% investor would not be hard to locate, he knew. It was easier than he had thought. Ronke, his wife, through means he did not know and didn't want to know, had piled up enough capital for another 30%. Before the week was over, Christopher had been approached by no less than five of his in-law's business associates, all of them foreign nationals who brought the remaining 10%. Finally, the hotel of his dream was born. It was a three-storey building of solid pageantry. Even the governor was present at the opening. There was plenty of speech-making and plenty to eat and drink. The atmosphere was one of general happiness with the happiest people being the major shareholders. Christopher's father-in-law was chairman, while Ronke was administrative manager. Each was to abandon all other business interests and devote all energy to the upliftment of the hotel's already soaring image.

For the first two years, things went on well. The hotel made maximum profit and everybody, management and customers alike, were satisfied. Then things began to go awry. Evidence of impropriety regarding Christopher's father-in-law's handling of the hotel finances began to surface. Customers began to complain about poor services. The heat was on. Cool and collected men would, under this kind of condition, keep their heads and rely on the force of reason. Not a woman. The pressure, however, was too much for Oluronke, Christopher's wife. She wanted out. She said she wanted her initial capital input back and was resigning from the hotel's management. She concluded by saying that she no longer had faith in her business ties with her father. Not only that, she never wanted her name associated with his again. She, in short, disowned her father, severing not only business ties but also blood ties. This was too much for her father. He could not bear to lose his only daughter.

What happened would never repeat itself again, he had said, trying to reassure his daughter, but she would not budge. She wanted out and that was that. When father realized that coaxing would not work, he changed tunes. He began to threaten. If she wanted out, she could leave, but she wasn't taking a penny away. Moreover, the articles of association did not permit anybody to withdraw his or her initial capital outlay upon leaving the services of the hotel. He solicited the help of the five other board members, who of course were his friends and thus loyal to him.

The next board meeting was held. Father and daughter threw brickbats at each other. They spat fire and grime. Then it was time to vote. Christopher reckoned that if he supported his wife, the votes would go in her favour. It would be 60% for her and 40% for her father. But doing this would have meant helping to break what he had helped to build. It would be tantamount to igniting the fire that would engulf the edifice whose idea he had conceived. That was why he voted for his father-in-law. Not because he liked the old man's policies or approved of his corruption. That vote, that singular act, was the only necessary one with which he solicited his wife's hatred. She would never forgive him, he knew. Not when he made love to her. Not when they went out together. Christopher knew in his heart of hearts that when the opportunity came, his wife would wreak her revenge upon him. What he did not know was when or how that would happen.

Life went back to the usual, with everyone going back to their old ways, except Oluronke. Father-in-law went back to his embezzling wheeling and dealing; son-in-law to his usual diligence and hard work; while his wife remained a passive onlooker. The events of the past few months had taken their psychological toll. She had lost her zeal. She no longer cared. She disregarded the old partners and branched into other business fields on her own, through which she accumulated fortunes.

Meanwhile, Christopher watched with sadness and helplessness. He was aware of his own faults. The major one being his blind ambition. He wanted Three Three Three to be the best hotel in the world. He wanted to be known as the patient, long-suffering doer. The all conquering conquistador. This was why he proposed to increase the floors in the hotel from its original three too twelve, a proposal which met with vehement disapproval from his father-in-law. It would amount to a waste of money, the man had said. If Christopher wanted to add more floors, he could proceed but then he would have to use his own money.

Because Christopher's burning ambition clouded all else, he accepted. He sank every kobo he owned into the project, and soon the task was completed. The edifice named "Three Three Three was raised from its former three floors to an imposing 12-storey edifice. Many people — staffers, clientele and all — were ecstatic. Christopher's father-in-law was not left out of the excitement. With his signature thick cigar resting in between his teeth, he bounced ecstatically around. Christopher didn't take all the credit, but shared it with his wife and father-in-law. No mention was made of the fact that he had used his personal funds for the project.

The newspapers attributed the success of the project to the foresight and hard work of the three major shareholders. This more than anything else incensed Christopher. His anger took the form of a resolution to continue increasing the height of Three Three Three to a whopping twenty-storey edifice, but his father-in-law again disapproved of him using hotel funds. This was not enough to deter Christopher. He loaned moneys, from banks, friends and credit co-operations. His father-in-law, however, was not the only one who was against the idea. So were the experts. They said the project was not feasible and that the foundation could not support what Christopher had in mind. But Christopher would not listen. His burning ambition would not let him. His dogged insensibility would not allow him to listen to any voice other than his own. He persisted. With the moral backing of those staffers, who for their own selfish reasons wanted the hotel raised, Christopher proceeded to build more floors. A one-storey building at the time it was called Three Three Three, soon became a thirteen-storey hotel and then fourteen, fifteen — yet retaining its beauty. It was tall and imposing. He had proved the cynics wrong. With time he might even surpass the twenty-storey target, he thought. And he continued to build. Then he got to the nineteenth and was already making plans to proceed on to the twentieth when it happened. The whole building, from the third floor up, came tumbling down. The losses were enormous, both in cash and in human lives. The police arrested Christopher and charged him for murder. Luckily, he was discharged and acquitted. He wasn't as lucky in matters of finance. He was completely bankrupt. He had not a kobo to his name. A mass of legal charges were brought up against him. Thousands of people sued him. And he had no money to hire a lawyer. He went to his wife for assistance, kneeling with cap in hand. She refused him help. Finally, with nowhere else to go, he went to his father-in-law, and it was he who bailed him out. He paid off every kobo Christopher owed but one without taking something in return. He obtained every one of Christopher's thirty percent shares in the hotel. Now the old man occupies the third floor of the three storey hotel, using it as office and abode. Christopher's wife lives on the second storey. There, she entertains her visitors, male and female. She no longer does any work. Christopher works in the hotel, tending the bar and kitchen, sleeping on the hard ground after each day's work but he isn't complaining.

Concluding the story he said in his own words: "I am aware of the existence of God. All that has happened is not in vain. Friend, I shall have the final laugh. And isn't that the one they say lasts longest?

Again, dear reader, I leave the judgment to you.

The Twins

Cactus plants do not grow in the rainforest. A camel is an animal of the desert and not the bush. The devil will never go to church to worship. It is impossible for a goat to mate a dog. A kennel is not the proper abode of a chicken. A senile old man has no business in the bar of a university student union restaurant. Yet, that was where I found him. The Sage — for that was what he called himself. And it was he who told me the story of the twins; the twins whom he claimed were his children.

It is worth recounting the events which led to my encounter with the old man. I had gone back to campus to collect my first degree certificate. Unfortunately for me, it was examination time. All the few friends I had left on campus were busy swotting.

I arrived the campus when all official business for the day had been concluded. I had no other option but to spend the night, and since I had no intention of turning myself into a nuisance to my friends who were preparing for their examination, I dropped my things in one of their rooms and went to the student union building bar for a bottle of drink or two. It was there I met him — the Sage.

"S.A.G.E," he spelt the words out, when I asked him what he had said. "Sage is the name," he had spat out in his drunken slur.

If his introduction was meant to elicit some form of response, he failed as I chose to ignore him and instead, ponder over the serenity of the environment, a far cry from when students, unburdened by the fear of fast approaching examination chose to shake the entire environment down with their bustling souls and youthful excitement. That I chose to ignore the old man did not appear to slow down his desire to start a conversation with me.

"They buried him today," he continued. They buried the son of a gun today and that's why I'm here. What else can a man do on the day of his son's burial than to drink himself silly," he slurred.

"Buried who?" I asked, convinced about his senility but wanting to humour him all the same.

Satisfied that he had won my attention, he moved his seat closer to mine and I was able to take in his profile. His head was a mass of grey hair. He had deep, sunken, bloodshot eyes. His nicotine-stained dentition was no surprise as he had not let the burning stick off his fingers since I got into the bar. His clothes were neatly laundered and must have been very expensive when he bought them.

"Barman, two more beers," he called out. "One for me and another for the young fella," he slurred, adjusting in his chair and using the butt of his burnt out "Gold Leaf" to light another cigarette. The bar tender brought the two bottles of beer, opened them and went back to his counter. It wasn't until then that the old man resumed his story. Which again I have taken the liberty to title *The Twins*.

***

"As I was saying," the old man slurred, "they buried him today, and since then, the land has known no peace. All over the place there is sorrow, tears and blood. Too much blood-letting, I tell you. They killed him and now they are killing one another."

He paused for effect, but since his words made no sense to me, I passed no comment. Seeing the look of bewilderment registered on my face, he said, "Oh sorry, you don't understand who I am talking about. I must start from the beginning. The very beginning.

"You see, I am a chief, a high chief, and the paramount ruler of the land of my birth. At the age of twenty-four, my father who was then the paramount ruler of the land, married for me a young ugly dame named Elizabeth. The wedding was elaborate, and everyone in the land was in attendance. Very soon after the wedding, father passed away and I ascended the throne. Thus, it was then that my two sons, the twins were born while I was on the throne.

"The birth of twins are supposed to be a thing of joy, for twins are believed to herald wealth, prosperity and all other good things of life. I, however, felt no joy at the birth of my twins because I believed I already had these things in abundance. The boys — for they were both boys — arrival was in my estimation, likely to result in a turn for my fortunes, I figured.

"At the back of my mind, however, an ominous feeling prevailed. There was again something about the physical characteristics of the boys that struck me as being very odd. They were the two most unidentical twins I had ever encountered. While Peter, the first one was light-complexioned and had Caucasian features, Nelson, the younger was as dark as charcoal, had Woolly hair and very thick lips.

"Ordinarily, this turn of events would have created an uproar in my land, a land that was used to the birth of very identical twins, but all forms of uproar was stifled by the simple realization than one of them Peter, was a carbon copy of my good old self while the other, Nelson, resembled his mother greatly. Any snide comment which might have occurred as a result of Nelson's ugliness was stifled. After all said and done, his mother was still the queen.

"An insight into the future personalities of the boys was also revealed at their birth. It was said that while Peter screamed his head off like one possessed, Nelson was as mute as a deaf.

"Naturally, it was Peter for whom I felt the greatest fondness and affection, and consequently it was on him that I showered all my love. His twin brother, I left in the care of his mother with whom at that time I was hardly on speaking terms with.

"As the boys grew, further differences began to emerge. Peter, for instance, turned out to be brilliant, quick-witted and gregarious. Nelson on the other hand was dull, dim-witted and introverted. Peter also was always on top of his class, whereas Nelson was always among the last three in the same class. Of course this development prompted not few visits from their class teachers who tried to argue that Nelson's academic ineptitude was as a result of the lack of warmth and affection on my part. I told them they were wrong, that brilliance was innate and certainly not a function of filial attention, and that I only had God to blame for giving me an ugly dullard as a son. Begone, I told them, feeling greatly angered at the ridicule which the boy had brought upon my royal home.

Of course, I was right, for why did it turn out that it was Peter who went to the university to study Politics while Nelson went to Agricultural School to learn goat herding. Peter knew that one day the land would be his to rule. With my assistance, he attended the best colleges to prepare himself for the arduous task. Nelson's animalistic instincts were sated with sitting among goats and other beasts of burden.

"And so the appointed day came for the investiture of the heir to the throne. Of course there was no doubt in any mind as regards whom the chosen one was to be. Peter, the one in whom I was well pleased was selected to mount the throne and preside over the affairs of his clansmen. This again, was unprecedented as the emergence of a ruler in my land was always effected only after the demise of an incumbent. But such was my love for Peter that I had to see him rule in my lifetime lest Nelson and his ugly mother started getting any funny ideas.

"The rites of investiture came and passed without any dissenting event of note. I was in fact rather pleasantly surprised at the active role Nelson played at his brother's enthronement, going as far as leading his band of farmers and hunters in doing the famous warrior dance. I was actually a little frightened when I first saw them, with their faces all painted with funny colours, with all of them wielding spears, bows, arrows and other kinds of cannibalistic artefacts. My apprehension must have been visible, because an aide whispered into my ear that what I was witnessing was the famous warrior dance, or fire dance, as it is elsewhere called.

"Fine dance I must say, but of course only fit for savages — savages who, if and when they posed any threat, could be easily subdued by the superior power of my chosen one.

"Yes, Peter's newly acquired power placed him in charge of the armoury. The armoury consisted of the gold and diamonds that were so bountiful in my land. My son, my chosen, had everything any man could ever ask for. That is why I still marvel at why he did it. Why he had to go and annoy those bunch of cannibals by ordering them to evacuate their farm lands. With that order, they would henceforth need passes to work their lands.

"In my entire journey throughout the land, I had never seen such a revolt that will match the one led by my other son, the ugly one. With the same weapons with which they used in the fire dance, Nelson and his band of bandits walked through the land and razed all in sight.

"What began as a riot in which many of Nelson's men were greatly defeated, escalated into a war of traumatic civil hostilities. And they killed Peter. It certainly was not Nelson, for he would not draw the blood of a brother, but some of his notorious followers. Peter was buried today.

"Too late. I now turn my filial attention to my other son, waiting for him to assume that which is his by right. But again they won't let him. Those same troublesome followers of who violently cut his brother off will not allow him to assume leadership of his father's land.

"Peter's men are causing disunity among themselves, while Nelson's followers are manning the throne. So, darkness reigns in the land with killings, maiming and other crimes being the order of the day.

"God, when will the bloodshed stop flowing?" he lamented, and kept quiet.

I looked at him and saw his eyes shut. There were tears in them.

"Sage," I called out, gently tapping him on the shoulder, but he didn't answer. "Sage," I again called out softly, only to be greeted with a snore. The senile old drunk had fallen asleep, and again I knew that this was one tale I had to figure out, just like you have to.

Johnny's Speech

I felt odd the first time I visited the Bamboo Bar. The feeling definitely was spured by the kinds of people I met there. All the young people who sat, danced or were chatting, seemed to possess some form of inner anger. It wasn't something that was audibly or visibly expressed, but it was there, somewhat bottled up in their subconscious. Their mode of dressing was also somewhat peculiar and almost uniform. Everybody, the ladies included, seemed to regard their dressing incomplete if there wasn't a jeans apparel in tow.

Marijuana was smoked openly, and I was able to catch a glimpse, in the dimly lit bar, of a couple deeply necking, and another in the throes of wild lovemaking. Surely this was a joint for Bohemians — a people often regarded as societal miscreants. I wondered what would happen if the police came visiting. There and then, I made a vow that I would never again visit the place. A vow occasioned by the fact that the lady, Angelina, whom I had taken there at her urging, had been gone for about an hour and appeared not to be in a hurry to come back. No, I lie. It was Angelina who had actually taken me to the Bamboo.

Angelina was a university dropout who lived very close to me. We had got talking one day and she invited me out. I had accepted and on that particular night she had come in the company of three of her friends — two male and a female — to pick me up in a Mercedes Benz, which most likely belonged to one of their parents. This story is of course not about Angelina, although she eventually came back and we had such a nice time talking and doing many other things.

It is about Johnny, the lead guitarist and singer of the resident band at the Bamboo Bar who I met on subsequent visits to the joint. Indeed, it is not a story in the real sense of the word. It is a speech which Johnny had drafted and always kept in the left pocket of his ragged jeans jacket.

Johnny is dread-locked, tall, slim, dark and handsome, and there is no doubt that many patrons of the female specie, who visit the Bamboo Bar do so on account of these attributes. He also has a good voice — a deep baritone — which brings out his rub-dub compositions in a mixture of ecclesiastical symphony and erotic magnetism.

He does drugs, I am certain, which is probably the reason why he always has this faraway look; the same look which didn't make me realize it was me he was addressing the night he called me out.

"Yo Brother, how ya like we jam?"

I was deeply engrossed in my thoughts and feeling very cross with Angelina who had left me at the Bamboo. The band members were busy packing up their things after playing their last number, the Asoca tune that I had not really paid attention to.

"Respect man," Johnny again said, moving towards the table where I sat.

"I and I was asking how ya dig we jam."

"Fine," I said. I wasn't in any mood for conversation with a stoned Bohemian.

"I can see you are not feeling very good," he said, changing from his Patois into impeccable English. I nodded, wishing he would get the cue and leave but he didn't.

"Must be the girl," he said, sitting beside me as he lit a spliff. "She didn't come, did she?"

I hadn't realised Johnny knew me, let alone my relationship with Angelina.

"They are all like that," he said, "every single one of them. Once you allow them to get a hold on you, you're finished. Never, trust women. Man, never. They're bloody leeches," he said, the last word coming out with a whiff of smoke.

"How do you mean?" I asked him.

"See? He doesn't know. Never trust women and never trust nobody because in the end, they'll always fuck you up! Me, I never trust nobody. I have been fucked up enough and I know." He paused, took a puff, looked around, then continued.

"I know that one day I'm gonna make it big. But then it gonna be alone because nobody, but nobody is ready to do nothing to help you make it big. It's gotta be you. It's gotta be solo, meeen! All these," he said, gesturing with his right hand round the bar, "is just a farce men, a prelude to the big thing, mere dress rehearsals. When big Johnny, hits the scene its gonna be with a big bang. You'll see brother, you'll see."

Having completely forgotten about my own problem, he launched into a tirade about himself — his past, his uncooperative family, his failed romantic exploits, his musical aspirations, the recording deal that almost came through but got "fucked up" because he wouldn't allow the studio director sodomize him, and so on.

"Babylon is never happy with talent, real talent. Babylon prefers the butt-lickers and the sycophants. But Jah spirit mighty much heavier than Babylon hypocrisy. Salaise I, Prince Tafari always triumphs in the end."

He spoke of another recording deal that was in the offing. The demo tape having been completed, it would herald the spiritual musical re-awakening of the century.

"Man, when that stuff comes off on vinyl, you'll see that everything else you've been listening to is kid's play, lyrical balderdash. Big Johnny is gonna turn on the drum and bass, and all dem pretenders are gonna cry like babies."

"When all that dream comes true, there is going to be a big musical launching for which Johnny has a speech specially prepared.

"It's always there *mon*, in the left pocket of my jacket lest Babylon come across it and spill the beans on me. A literary masterpiece I call it. It's gonna keep all the industry captains glued to their seats. On that big day, the whole of Babylon is going to be spellbound."

He fished into his pocket and whisked out a sheaf of folded sheets, rough in appearance probably on account of being carried around for too long. On the top of the first page was written in bold letters JOHNNY'S SPEECH. It is this speech, dear reader, that you are reading presently.

****

Ladies and gentlemen, I welcome you to this top musical event of the decade. I expect that so far you have all had a pretty good time courtesy of all those who have had the honour of making speeches before me. I am, however, very sorry that I will have to temporarily put a stop to your good time. Why? Because tonight I am finally free to tell the truth. Because unlike all those who had come to this podium to talk, I don't have to lie anymore. I see you shifting uneasily in your seats. Relax, you haven't heard nothing yet. First, let me start by debunking a few of the lies already told. It began with my mother — my sweet-faced mother who — came to tell you all, how she had always known that I was gonna be a big music star.

You lied Mama; Mama you lied. Or maybe you didn't. Maybe you actually did know. And you did encourage me, didn't you? You did say so yourself, how much you encouraged my artistic ambitions. I am sure by encouragement you mean the number of times you called me right in the middle of some very important composition, to sweep the floor, fry eggs, slice okro or perform some equally stupid chore. Or the numerous occasions when you shut the kitchen at my face because I refused to go to school. Some encouragement! Mama, you knew quite well my star qualities each time you referred to me as a neer-do-well, and compared me to all my primary school classmates who were already university graduates and had good jobs and a family to boot. Thanks Mama for all the encouragement.

And you too Papa. How can I not acknowledge your support and encouragement? Just a while ago you were up here with a "that's my boy" grin covering your entire face. Where has the grin disappeared to? You couldn't have forgotten so early Papa, how many times you threatened to disown me. The many occasions on which you broke my guitars which you claimed I was using to disturb your peace. Countless times Papa, you threw them and my things out of the house in the middle of the night, urging me to go and join my raggamuftn friends. Now you say to yourself, "That's my boy". No papa, I ain't your boy. You know your boy and I know him and he knows himself. Charley, my junior brother. He's here too today, I think. It is funny, this thing we call human memory.

Charley has forgotten how a few months ago he said he was ashamed to be seen with me. No longer ashamed is he, eh? Charley, yes Papa, Charley's your boy. Or have you forgotten that he was the one who always did the chores. Who read Law like you wanted him to. Isn't he the one who now works as your junior partner? And yes, my friends too. Remember the number of times you laughed behind my back? Called me a drunken layout, offering your handouts as though I was some kind of beggar. You can't laugh anymore, can you? No, you can't. You know why? Because, henceforth it's going to be me doing the laughing. And you know one more thing? My laughter is going to be towards the direction of the banks.

Ah! My girlfriends, I count about six of you here. I wonder what this world is coming to. Yes, I know. I have always known that while I was good enough to croon serenades to you, I was never good enough to take home to meet mum. I had no future, so you said, Ireti. Bukky was more dignifted in her silence, while offering me her nubile body. I bet he doesn't know the guy in whose B.M.W you are always seen cruising. Your ftancee, you called him, didn't you? Yet he doesn't know you are here. Perhaps you think I didn't see you pointing and laughing derisively at me as you both sped past me at the Bus Stop. "He's just a toaster," so you said about the big pot-bellied joker who almost caught us at it in the flat he rented for you. "He's just a toaster", you had told the perverter of young girls in your whimpering baby voice. So what am I now? Jezebel? A stove? No, baby, you know what I am? A kettle, boiling from the recesses of my depth. A microwave, sizzling hot and ready to roast. Young lady, I'm a rocket aimed at the skies and I see you wanting to be par of that flight. No honey, stick to sugar daddy".

There are a few more liars here tonight. I see the agent who once said the best my voice could come up with was a funeral dirge. The aunty who pointed a cruciftx at me saying my locks were a manifestation of Satan. I am too tired to tell you all how I feel about you. So what I'll do is to go home and sleep and I urge you all to do the same. But I know you won't. Instead you will prefer to stay here or go to some other places where you could tell each other how rude and ungrateful I have been and what strategies you can map out to effect my fall. But I tell you this, whatever tree Almighty Jah watereth from mount Zion, remains evergreen till the kingdom comes. Good night.

I pondered over Johnny's speech a great deal and wondered if he would be able to deliver such a devastating address, if and when he ultimately realized his ambitions. Time and the sweet taste of success, I am sure, would have mellowed down the hurt he felt within. I also realized that one of the commonest traits in this land, both as individuals and collectively as a nation, is that we tend to forgive and forget quite easily. Now I wonder whether that is a vice or a virtue. Once again you'll have to find the answer yourself.

Megida

This tale I am about to recount was told me by a friend's uncle. This friend of mine — my unemployed friend — had one Saturday urged me to accompany him to visit his uncle, a jailed politician, at the jail house.

Uncle B — that was what my friend called his uncle — was in high spirits as we spoke to him across the steel bars. He joked and gave a deep throaty laugh as he asked us questions about the outside world. Just as we were set to leave, he related this tale. I have tried to tell Uncle B's story as best as I can. There's much to learn from this tale. I urge you to read and learn from it.

****

"You need to have seen my father's mansion a short while ago. Even those who did not really have eyes for aesthetics conceded that it was an architectural masterpiece. Truth be told, my father bought and or inherited this edifice and masterpiece from a white man. But so did every other person who possessed some form of abode in our neighbourhood. In the entire length and breadth of the neighbourhood, it was outright impossible to find a house that matched ours in terms of size and beauty.

"The story is often told that when my father bought or inherited the house from the white man, it was as large but not as beautiful as it was. They say it was through my father's hard work and providence from God that our house rose to it's status. First and foremost, my father was a farmer. It thus came as no surprise to those who knew him well when he tilled the land in his large compound to cultivate the most beautiful flowers in the neighbourhood. The flowers served a dual purpose. The first was for aesthetic purpose — to beautify the surroundings. The second was for financial purpose. Folks came from far and near to purchase some of my father's flowers. And in no time he began to make substantial amounts from the proceeds of the sale of these flowers.

"Thus began the rise in the fortune of both my father and his mansion. As things began to improve and the place began to expand, so also the volume of work increased. He thus decided to hire a man to help around the house.

"It was here that my father made his first mistake. Although the official designation of the man my father hired was to be night and day guard, however, his duties and the roles that were his to play were not clearly mapped out. Thus, while the man was supposed to be manning the gates solely, it came to be that at times he was found watering the plants, sweeping the floor, washing the dishes and even cooking in the kitchen. This state of affairs of course led to some conflict. Our man was found on many occasions having clashes with the gardener, the houseboy and of course our dearly beloved cook. This was probably the reason why the first holder of the office of night and day guard did not stay too long with us. So did the second.

"By the time my father had hired the third night and day guard, things had begun to cool off and the *Megad** had come to be recognized as more or less a permanent fixture in our household.

"Can this story be complete without due mention being made of our third *Megad*? Our course, no. Jacobs was his name. Jack

---

*Megad is the local pronunciation of "main guard" in Nigerian parlance, usually referring to a watchman.

Jacobs was a strikingly handsome young man who took as wife a lovely bride while he was *Megad* in our mansion. It is important to note that it was while Jacobs was our *Megad* that father made a discovery that was to change the life of everybody in our household.

"One day, while my father was busy tilling the land at our backyard, he came across a spot where it appeared as though something had been hidden there. Upon digging up the soft mass of earth, my father found to his utter amazement that in there had been hidden an inexhaustible mass of golden chandeliers.

"'Hurry,' my father shouted, unable to contain his joy, and we all rushed out to see what had been the cause of his outburst. Out there, we were confronted by the largest quantity of chandeliers any one of us had even seen.

"From that day onwards, our lives changed. At every nook in our home hung a chandelier. Gold seemed to flow from everywhere. The excess, we sold off at maximum profit. Yet the stock could not be depleted. Nobody cared, we were all having a nice time.

"Meanwhile, Jacobs had begun to involve himself in some excesses. One day he went to the boys-quarters and fought with everybody there because he had a grudge to settle with one of the occupants. But nobody paid attention to him; we were all busy spending money while he went about making trouble.

"It, however, soon got to the stage where his excess could no longer be tolerated. He was getting more troublesome and even resorted to telling lies. He also became very rude. One day, he walked up to my father and said it to his face that my father was not a realistic person. That was it. Nobody was prepared to have any more of his impertinence. He had to go. And go he did. To be replaced by Mamudu, a no-nonsense *Megad* who though that the fact that he was a no-nonsense person meant that he would be loved by all. A mistake. A costly one indeed in that it was a cat, a mere dim-witted pussy cat that scratched his face and made him leave our home, I think, in annoyance.

"Baxon, a chubby round fellow who had been helping Mamudu along took over as *Megad* and nobody seemed to remember what he did or didn't do. The only significant thing for which he is remembered is that his exit paved way for Megida about who this story is really about, to mount guard at my father's gate.

"Now, Megida didn't want the job. The job was thrust upon him. Perhaps again it is worth recounting the circumstances which led to this state of affairs.

"Baxon was called back to his village. It was said that certain matters needing his urgent attention had cropped up. Something to do with his father's poultry farm. Anyway, a week to his departure, my father let out word that he was in dire need of another *Megad*. Perhaps due to the fact that my father's generosity in remunerating his domestic staff, especially his *Megad*, was well-known in our neighbourhood, applications came pouring in. In order to make things orderly, my father named a date on which he intended to personally interview each applicant. It was on this particular day that Megida came to our household. He claimed that he was not there to be interviewed but to merely watch proceedings. Some people might wish to argue that someone who came to watch proceedings could have probably done so from afar, and not at such a close range. But I don't agree. Megida probably stood at the head of the line because he thought that from there, he would be able to view proceedings better. Not very smart, you would say but Megida never made any pretence about being smart.

"Anyway Megida was at the head of the queue and one good look at him by my father was enough for him to give Megida the job and drive all the other applicants away without even bothering to interview them. This my father did in spite of the several feeble protestations from Megdia who became our *Megad*.

We later asked our father why he took such a decision which appeared rash. Why had he, we asked him, given the job to Megida whom he hardly knew instead of a certain old man in the neighbourhood, whom despite his few shortcomings, had been tried, tested and found to be efficient in similar areas of human endeavour.

"Our father, in answer to our question, gave two reasons. The first was that the old man was too desperate in wanting the job and it showed. My father said in a case where there was a commodity and two customers, it was better to give the commodity to the least interested customer. Logical isn't it?

"The other reason, my father gave was that, in spite of the fact that the old man had not yet been appointed, he had begun mouthing things that, had it been a country was involved, it would have amounted to treason. One of such things the old man blabbed about said was vowing to find out the source of the chandeliers and the use to which they were put. The "Nosey Parker." Having learnt the truth about the old man, we were so incensed that our immediate reaction was to seek him out of his abode and stone him to death. But our father's wise counsel prevailed — better to leave him alive as a frustrated person than to kill him; leave him alive and deny him what he seeks.

"The business of seeking out a *Megad* was thus completed. We all went back to our different businesses and proceeded to watch how Megida would fare at his new job. He did a great job. In the first six weeks of his being appointed, armed marauders visited our abode six times! On another occasion, he mistakenly left his burning cigarette around a high inflammable liquid. The result was that my father's entire orchard was burnt down. Now, that wasn't the only time Megida's chain smoking was responsible for such kind of disaster.

"Despite all of this, my father refused to send Megida away. Why? 'This man is going to ruin you if you don't to something about him,' we complained to our father.

"But my father's reply was always the same. 'There's something about that man that makes it impossible for me to sack him. Something about him makes me always want to protect him, to baby him. I just can't bear to hurt him. Even if he's not doing too well, I think he should be encouraged, and not driven away.'

"It was true. There was indeed something about Megida that made you want to reach out and touch him. He possessed a certain vulnerability which made most people want to be his father or mother or big brother or sister or friend. Most people, not everybody. Some folks saw this quality in Megida too and decided to turn it to their own advantage. Megida's vulnerability made him highly susceptible to manipulation, they figured out. And they were right.

"Megida's so-called friends began to bombard our domicile with reckless abandon. We would then discover soon after they had left that one object or the other was missing. We would ask Megida what he knew about it and he would reply in his thin voice, 'Walahi Talahi, I don't know anything about it.'

"And we all would believe him. We could vow using both the Quran and Bible that Megida was no thief. Perhaps he aided and abetted. Either that or he simply looked the other way while his friends carried on their nefarious activities. This we found out when we all went on a short vacation, leaving Megida to man the fort. We came back to find out that the entire house had been stripped bare. Nothing was left, save the chandeliers. Megida's friends had carted everything away.

"Naturally, we again asked Megida what he knew about the theft. He lit a stick of Benson, bit into a kolanut, looked up and said, 'Ze good Lord knows Zat I know nothing about Ze theft.'

"That was it! Nobody was prepared to have anymore of Megida. A few of my uncles came and whisked Megida to the police station. After this, they took it upon themselves to personally man the gates. But the damage had been done. There was nothing left. The looters had done their worst and none of them was anywhere to be found. No, that is not true. We found some of Megida's friends and locked them up. In our anger at the time, we did not care whether they were part of the looters who had fled the neighbourhood and there was simply nothing we could do about it.

"Meanwhile, we were feeling the crunch. Even sales of the chandeliers could not redeem us. It was revealed to us that chandeliers, even if they were gold were not worth as much as they used to be. Poverty was the word. Poverty and hunger now reigned in a house that had known nothing other than opulence and wealth. Just as we were learning to adjust; trying to find our feet in the new dispensation, they came out with a bang — the law enforcement agents, those paid to dispense justice. They had monitored and scrutinized Megida's every move since he became our *Megad*, so they said. Carefully, they had gone through the minutest details of his life — public and private — and had found nothing incriminating. The verdict: Megida was not guilty.

"Anywhere that you are today, Megida, congratulations and thanks for a job well done.

Sunshine (For Ray)

"Sunshine, was undoubtedly the prettiest maiden in our village. It is hard to start describing her beauty. Her beauty was such that spoke for itself. You needed to see her to fully appreciate God's work.

"But Sunshine was a bastard. Nobody knew her father. Sorry, nobody knew her real father. It is claimed that around the time that she was conceived, her mother was consistently sleeping with four men. It was therefore a difficult matter indeed to determine which of the four men was Sunshine's real father. The men too did not help matters. Each claimed paternity of the angelic beauty.

"In the end, it was quietly agreed that each of the four men should be regarded as Sunshine's father. Since she was staying with her mother who in turn lived alone, it was agreed that each of the four men could pay her visits whenever they liked. A specific role was also set for each man to play in the girls' life. One was to be responsible for her education, another for her feeding, another for her clothing, and the last was to screen all her suitors when the time arrived for sunshine's wedding.

"The man who emerged out of this arrangement with what seemed to be the largest share of the responsibilities was Chidi, a heavily moustached man who was well known for his natty dressing. Chidi, of course, had no cause to complain. He could shoulder the responsibility. He was a man noted for his large capacity for work, and of course his efforts yielded fruits. He was by no means a poor man even though his life history would have read like a rags to riches classic.

"Around this area, one must be pardoned if the story begins to switch a bit from Sunshine to Chidi, one of her fathers.

"Chidi was a very remarkable man in one aspect. Friendliness. In this area, he seemed to be an enigma. His capacity for friendship was unmatchable. Nowhere in our village could a man be found who had so many friends in high places and as many in low places at the same time. Chidi was loved by many and hated by many. Why?

"Chidi was a policeman by profession. The nature of his job was such that he had to step on a few toes at different times. In this manner, he came about his many enemies.

"To be sure, Chidi indeed had a choice. If he didn't want enemies, there was something he could do — to simply look the other way when a crime was being committed. That way, he could keep all his friends and acquire no enemy. But Chidi, as said earlier, was a man of unparalleled patriotism and dedication to duty. He had such great deal of respect for the law that was rare to find within young men in our village. He was fired by a patriotic zeal to see our village become a better place to live in. In this one aspect, Chidi would not compromise. And that was what they wanted him to do.

"Certain folks wanted Chidi to sell his ideals for a pot of porridge — to look the other way while they carried out their shady deals. But he would not compromise nor live by their terms. Chidi knew that it was better to die for the things you believed in than live with the things you didn't. In the end, he had to be silenced. One lovely morning while he sat at his ancestors' shrine in worship, an unknown coward crept behind him and hit him with a deadly weapon. He died alright. But he didn't die. How? Why? Because although Sunshine's paternity had still not been established. After Child's death, Sunshine came to be recognized as the product of his passion.

"Sunshine had watched her father and imbibed most, if not all, of his ideals. After the initial period of mourning, she proceeded to relentlessly work towards accomplishing those ideals her father believed in; those things for which he had lived and died for. She also made a vow to find out who her father's killers were. Not an easy task for a fatherless girl, you would say, but Sunshine wasn't exactly fatherless, she still had three fathers left, plus a host of many other sympathizers.

"With these as her armour, she embarked on the job she had set for herself with vigour. To some though, she was better off passive — those who had thought that by killing Chidi, they would be free to pursue, unperturbed, their nefarious activities. Sunshine had put a lie to their line of thought. What else could they do then? Kill the three other fathers? No, that wouldn't do. Sunshine was the real enemy. Even if they killed her other fathers, could they kill her teeming sympathizers? No way. An aura surrounded her. So what did they do?

"It was common knowledge that every Monday, Sunshine went to the village stream to take a bath. On such mornings, many left their various tasks to catch a glimpse of the lovely maiden in her nudity. Although Sunshine was privy to this, she, however, never bothered to cover herself up. She was proud of her beautiful form.

"One particular Monday, Sunshine came out looking more beautiful than ever, and as usual, every one abandoned their duties to catch a glimpse of her — market women, school children, farmers, policemen and the likes. This was the moment the killers of her father were waiting for. They rushed to the village chief's palace to inform him.

"'Kabiyesi,' they chorused in unison, 'Sunshine, if you don't act quickly, is going to throw our village into jeopardy.'

'What do you mean?' the Kabiyesi asked them.

'Word of mouth cannot describe what we have seen. You need to see things for yourself.'

"And so the Kabiyesi hurriedly dressed up. Wearing his beads and beaded crown, followed the petitioners to town. They took him to the farms and he saw that the farmers were not there. They went to the market place and saw no traders. To the schools, they took the chief, all were as silent as graveyards.

"'What is the cause of all these?' the chief asked. 'How is Sunshine responsible for this?'

"But the petitioners only kept mute. When they found their voice, they said, 'You shall see for yourself exalted one,' and took the chief to the village stream. There they saw the entire village — market women who had neglected their wares; school children who had neglected their books; farmers who had neglected their machetes and hoes. There, they all stood applauding, the naked beauty of Sunshine as she swam in the village stream. All this the king saw for himself and was visible annoyed.

"'How dare you, Sunshine, distract folks from their duties thus?'

"Even as he said this, it was glaring that he too was disturbed; that sunshine's nakedness was getting to him.

"'Will you put something on quickly,' he again shouted.

"Sunshine complied in obedience to the chief. But the damage had already been done. In order to please the petitioners, the chief knew he would have to punish Sunshine and so had to quickly think up a punishable offence. He wasn't dim witted; he knew that there was a standing law which forbade public disturbance. Well, he thought, what Sunshine had just engaged in constituted public disturbance of sorts. That was it. She would be punished for public disturbance; for constituting herself into a public nuisance.

"Thus, the chief decreed that Sunshine was to stay indoors for six months; that she was not to be seen in public for the duration of half a year. The petitioners were glad. This was the fulfilment of their heart's desires. They were sure that if sunshine spent six months out of public glare, she was sure to become a forgotten person. Other beauties would emerge and be celebrated. By the time Sunshine came out of her banishment, she would be old, forgotten and ugly. But they were mistaken.

"The chief, having retired to his palace could find no rest of mind. He knew in his heart of hearts that Sunshine had done nothing wrong. He was known for his magnanimity. He was aware that by the singular action he took against Sunshine, he had soiled his reputation as a magnanimous chief. In no time, while the petitioners were still busy drinking palm wine and celebrating Sunshine's banishment, the chief came out to say the banishment was over. The din of approval that greeted this announcement was such that was heard villages away. The chief had again proven that he was a man of the people.

"'Long live, the Chief. Long live Sunshine, the villagers chorused.

Trust Sunshine, she was sure to come out in style. She delayed her coming out by a full one week by which time people were dying of anticipation.

"She came out draped in silken robes and was as beautiful as ever. But she had added a few more attributes — class and style. Sunshine was a qualitative lady. Perhaps, this was what prompted a few observers to say she had lost her drive — her ruggedness, doggedness, and her rigid determination to find her father's murderers.

"Rumour even had it that she already knew them but was in no hurry to divulge the knowledge.

"But that would be unfair. Sunshine would never keep the secret of her father's murderers away from her teeming admirers. Perhaps she doesn't know yet, some said, trying to defend her. But someday she'll find out. And then it will no longer be a secret because she sure will sing...."

Letter to Father

When you are drinking, you seldom realize that you are hungry. It is only after you are done with the drinking spree that the hunger pangs hit you with a bang. Then you realize that you have to find something to eat.

The pangs hit me one such night, and I sought through the length and breadth of town, a place where I could assuage the anger of the stomach worms.

It was a bean cake seller who eventually came to my rescue. She was noted for her been cakes which she sold along with loaves of bread to bail out night-combers such as I, from the cold pangs of naked hunger, stomach ulcer or even death.

The oil-soaked shafts of paper in which she wrapped the bean cakes were insignificant then. It wasn't until the next morning that I took note of them.

The sheets were seven in number, and on them was a letter written by someone who simply signed, "Sanya". This letter revealed Sanya as a man dissatisfied with life. He was a very angry youth who felt alienated in the scheme of things. He had chosen his father to vent his spleen upon. What he wrote in that letter represents the feelings of many of today's youths. I have decided to share its contents, aptly titled, "Letter to Father."

****

Dear Father,

I received your letter today and I must confess I was very upset by its contents. In it your raised several allegations against me which I ftnd disconcerting. You pointed out that I have turned out to be a big disappointment and that you are ashamed having me as your only son. You claimed in your letter, and quoting the scriptures, that I had not done you and mother sufftcient honour, and that I was therefore bound to go the way of my biblical forebears — a veiled insinuation that I shall not have long life.

Father I accept the allegations and insinuations in good faith and was going to allow the matter to rest except for the fact that I realized that certain records need to be set straight. Daddy, I must let you know that the feeling of being let down is mutual, and in case you do not know, let me tell you that I have ceased to have respect for you a very long time ago. It is my opinion that your senile memory may require some re urging on the incidents which led to this state of affairs. Earlier in your life father, remember you were the head teacher in one of the most popular secondary schools in the land. The tales we heard about you then revealed that you were the embodiment of school discipline and that you made a real success of your vocation. I remember it being said that the most irresponsible, obstinate and dull student, when brought tc your school, was transformed into an academic marvel. You were indeed doing great service to your nation.

I remember that time when the powers that be felt that you had done enough service to the nation, and that it was indeed time that you did yourself some service too. They didn't come out and say so but it was all there in the appointment you were given. Father you were made the Education Commissioner of our great state. In spite of my youth at the time father, I knew that that kind of appointment came once in one's life time. It's an opportunity for the appointed to make his own grand entry into the world of riches and luxury, and to inscribe his name on the lush walls of fame and power.

The day the appointment was made stands out in my memory. The ecstatic din which overtook our home was too much. That night I found it difftcult to sleep. All forms of vision kept passing through my brain. Even though I was just in forth form then, the fact did not in any way limit the scope of my dreams.

I dreamt father, I dreamt. I dreamt that in no time we would move out of the ramshackle in which we lived in and move into government quarters. I was also certain that in no time at all, you would have built a mansion; a real architectural masterpiece whose frontage would be adorned by a fleet of cars. There, our needs would be attended to by a dozen or more servants. I dreamt of annual vacations to Europe and America. I knew for sure that after completing secondary school, I would be off to Oxford for my ftrst degree. The next port of call would then be Harvard University, from where I would proceed to Patrice Lumumba — no, that is in a communist country — Howard , for my doctorate. I dreamt of coming back to the land to head the multinational company which by then you would have founded. I would marry the daughter of another commissioner, a successful businessman, the governor, of even the head of state. I dreamt of a big ceremony attended by the president himself, ministers, diplomats, governors and all the who's who in the land. After that we would have our honeymoon in the Bahamas. So, I dreamt. My spouse and I would then retire to your third or so mansion where we would live happily ever after.

You of course you know, don't you, how those dreams turned out? They were mere fantasies. Common flights of fancy. Why? Because the dumb-headed pastor and ex-principal that God gave to me as a father blew his chances. You, father messed up like no one had ever done in the history of our great country. Father, you had the audacity to carry your Christian and Marxist/Socialist doctrines into the sanctifted walls of the bureaucracy. Who didn't warn you father? Who didn't advice you?. Twice, I overheard your bosom friends telling you that people did not go about things in the way that you were going about them; that although a man needed ideals, an ideal bank account was more important. I am ware of the fact that your kinsmen practically begged you. They urged you to, at least stash something away for the rainy day. After all, said your relatives, government offtce was not something to last a lifetime. One needed something to fall back on.

But you wouldn't budge. Yours was unprecedented. It was as though you came from Mars or some equally remote planet.

I recall when I got our neighbour's daughter, Sheri, pregnant. I had pleaded with her to get an abortion, but her parents, upon hearing about this, spat blue murder and declared that, "Awa shild weel not haj abosion." (Our child will not have an abortion)

"Oh Sanya, when are you going to get responsible? Don't you want me to cuddle my grandchild in my life time?" Mother had wailed.

And you, dear father, ought to have sided up with me on the matter. Your singular opposition to the marriage would have saved the day. Remember what you said? No? I'll remind you. "It is the express commandment of God that no human life shall be taken and that unborn foetus which that poor girl is carrying in her womb constitutes human life." There was no mansion father, you know too well. For you had to move with your family into a dilapidated room and parlour apartment.

Humiliation and my new status as husband and expectant father would not allow me move in with you. So with the loan obtained from friends, I moved into, with Seri, a one room apartment, devoid of burglary proof, lacking potable water and characterized by incessant power cuts, and inhabited by hoodlums, touts, prostitutes and other miscreants of the society.

That was what you did to me, father. While you know perfectly well what injury you did to my Psyche, you can not know the inner turmoil that I went through during this whole period. But of course, one would have thought that was enough, but no, there was more to come.

After a short while, your friends believed that perhaps, the Spartan life you were living might have wizened you up a bit. Shocked and perhaps touched by the level of abject poverty to which your existence had ascended, they put their heads together and though of a way to bring you back up. What they came up with this time was a real live wire. They made you a special adviser on some very obscure matters. The unspoken instructions given to you were explicit enough for even the most dumb-headed of men:

> "You do not have any responsibilities. Just have this office and this official car and steal as much money as you can. Attend a few meetings when you have the time and when you get bored, call a press conference and repeat our party's manifestos."

That was all, nothing more, no nothing. Father, all my former hopes immediately became rekindled after this appointment — the Oxford dream, the multinational companies, etc., etc. I would resign, of course, I had reasoned. I mentally drafted my resignation letter in which I told my boss to shove it deep where it belonged.

But you blew it again, father. Father, you allowed Marx and Lenin to do untold damage to your head. And then it happened that morning, when I tuned the radio and heard, "I Brigadier...." thus, bringing an end to you and your friends' regime. I also felt, at that point, like committing a mutiny — mutineering against God for giving me a father like you.

I had always felt that you knew all these but your letter which I received today shows you don't. You requested for honour and obedience, dear father. I assure you that you shall get it in the coming years when everything would be free. Marxists, anarchists and all other categories of people whose dream of a property-less world would have come true shall converge in Russia to commemorate the anniversary of one of their great mentors, Karl Marx. On that day, the Nigerian delegation shall put up your name for honourable mention. Now, isn't that enough honour?

Your Son, (Sgd)
/Sanya

Anita

This job hunting business could sometimes get risky. The attendant problems of unemployment as they manifest in societal disdain, consists of being constantly broke. Ceaseless idleness can, to a certain extent, be dealt with. But when one's physical existence is actually threatened as a result of being unemployed, then there is some cause for alarm.

The letter inviting me for an interview at an oil company stated explicitly that those who arrived one minute later than the stipulated 9.00am would not be allowed into the interview hall. I had to sleep in the riverine town no doubt. And so I had booked a hotel room in a downtown part of the city. A hotel room? The entire hotel housed only two bathrooms. Bedsheets were soiled with oil and semen.

The mosquito net revealed large holes in several places. There was difficulty in sleeping. What with the constant noise which the mosquitoes made in my ears and the loud noise from the dimly lit bar where the whores and pimps converged and engaged in a drinking spree.

Sleep mercifully came, that is, after I had checked my wrist watch and saw that the time was 4.00 a.m. It was the kind of slumber in which one was never too sure if he was actually asleep or awake.

Waking up was a relief which occurred at about 6:30 a.m. I got dressed, gathered my and proceeded to the company which had invited me for the interview.

Of course, I had at the back of my mind that this was just another job interview. Everybody knew that such things were mere formalities which the companies underwent so as to give the impression that they cared about society. Usually, those to be selected for the job were already known. In most cases, they didn't undergo any interview. All they needed was a complimentary card signed by somebody whose name commanded respect as regards the power or wealth, or both, that the signee wielded.

One, however, attended this interviews just in case something had gone wrong with the status quo and some people decide to do the right thing just for once, the way they are supposed to be done.

These thoughts, however, provided no consolation, as over five hundred of us attended this interview which I learnt was for only four vacant posts. This again raises the question as regards the sadistic nature of our employers... over five hundred people for four vacant positions! And as if that wasn't enough psychological punishment on its own, the panel decided to conduct oral interviews for each of the shortlisted applicants one at a time. There were some who were lucky, their names appeared early enough on the list. I wasn't so lucky. My name was among the last eight, which meant that by the time I was called, it was a little after six in the evening. The panel had risen about thrice to proceed on such mundane things as lunch break, coffee break, and breathtaking break. I could not afford the luxury of a break because I only had my exact fare back home. Twice, anyhow, I bummed cigarettes from one security guard who seemed to, without my telling him, understand my plight.

Why didn't I leave? You don't come this close and then quit. You don't begin to smell a job and then run away because some capitalist blue coats are wasting your time. Moreover, this was the kind of class one so desperately wished to join. So what the heck. You stayed and weathered the storm. Which I did but which still didn't make me feel any better, for one of the panellists kept insinuating that I was a radical and therefore couldn't be entrusted with maintaining the status quo if employed.

"We can't stand employees under our payroll criticizing company policies," they argued.

This was all because I had made mention of some Marxist literature I had read, upon enquiry of my reading habits. Anyway I left the interview, hungry, angry and feeling very very low. A feeling which heightened upon my arrival at the motor park, only to discover that there was no single vehicle available. What was there to do? I was at total loss. The ramshackle hotel in which I had spent the previous night was out of the question because I had run out of cash. What else was there to do? Spend the night at a police station? Tales of folks stranded who had strayed to police stations only to end up being charged for some ill-conceived offence came flooding my mind. No, I wasn't ready to be a guest of the police. Not on any terms.

As I stood staring into outer space, a trailer came tottering towards where I stood, dry dust heavy on its tail, and I sought to move for cover. As it sped past, I waved it down, my hands flailing, with my lungs almost bursting with shouts of "stop, stop." It did stop. Surprise, it was headed for where I was going. I got in after negotiating with the driver to pay half the normal fare which conventional vehicles charged. There was another occupant apart from the driver on the passengers side of the trailer.

Somehow we got talking, with the driver chipping in. Alone on the road at night, you sometimes become friends with people who are complete strangers. But being friends didn't stop Alfred, for that was the name of the other passenger, from chiding Musa the driver when he partook of locomotive over-zealotry. Alfred as it turned out had suffered the loss of the friend of a close friend, Anita, from a road accident.

A university graduate, also unemployed in the sense of formal employment, but a salesman for his brother's tie and dye wares, Tony, Alfred's friend, was constantly on the road. This was a story Alfred had told everybody he met, who cared to listen. It is therefore possible that you may have met Alfred and he has told you this tale. If so, forgive me for the repetition. If you haven't, then here is Alfred's story. Again, I urge you to make whatever sense you may from it. Hear Alfred.

****

"I don't think they make women like Anita anymore. A girl of unspeakable beauty, Anita was the embodiment of humility even though she came from a background of immensely wealthy parents. It was this simplicity, this humble background which attracted my friend Tony to her. Tony was an idealist, somebody who possessed a rare gift of childhood innocence. From a very humble background, Tony felt total disregard for material possessions. He found it difficult to understand negative states of mind such as envy, petty jealousy and hatred. He felt it was the quest for material possessions that led to these state of mind. Man was born naturally good, he always argued, it was the quest for earthly survival that turned him into something no better than animals. And so with Anita, Tony formed a cult of peace and camaraderie within the campus. But their dreams were not limited to their campus days. It was the goal of these two that one day, the crusade shall extend to the outside world.

"The fad caught on campus and I was one of the confraternity's first converts. We were a non-religious, non-political group, distributing pamphlets containing the words of great men who had one time or the other denounced war and the attendant elements which militated against world peace. Gandhi, Mandela, and even Nietzsche's words were the slogans we carried round the campus.

It was an irony of great dimension, that those two people who did so much for the attainment of inner peace, knew no peace themselves. The couple continued to encounter antagonism from members of their family who frowned on their relationship. Anita's because of Tony's humble background. Tony's because Anita came from a different tribe.

"It is a tribute to the resilient spirit of man that this relationship weathered all the storms in spite of several actions which could have seen to its end.

"Anita's parents stopped paying her fees while Tony's aged mother brought out her flat breasts from the weathered loincloth she tied around her emaciated frame to plead with Tony to stop his act of "socio-political disgrace.

"None of these intimidations worked. The relationship blossomed with the couple growing fonder of each other. By the approach of graduation, both families had begun to accept the true situation of things. These were two people who genuinely cared about each other. Nothing could break their love. Peace was made with the families and all had begun to look forward to a bright future for them when tragedy struck. Anita went home one weekend and never returned. On her journey back to school, a trailer ran into the chauffeur-driven Mercedes Benz which was bringing her back. She died instantly along with the driver. Her skull was crushed. The driver of the trailer, a lone occupant, survived without the tiniest scratch.

"It was sad," concluded Alfred with mist in his eyes. "Anita Azubuike, may her soul rest in peace. She didn't deserve the kind of death she died."

****

I was no longer listening. My mind worked upon the unfairness of the entire world system. Nasty people lived, even till old age, while young, promising people got killed in undeserving ways. And then the roads. Why did it always extract its pound of flesh by claiming innocents? Do the priests always fail in their appeasement of Ogun? My mind continued to query but registered one little fact from Alfred's continued rambling. Tony and Anita had a love child.

After Tony's story, Musa sobered up by driving within the limits of maximum safety. The rest of the journey was done in silence. Once, we stopped to eat some *suya* and soft drinks. But the tension remained high. Somehow, Anita's story had touched us all. I do not know to what extent with Musa, but for me, the tragedy has seeped into the very marrow of my bones.

Nothing significant remained of that journey except that I finally got home at about 2.00 a.m to meet a very worried mother who had waited up for me, and who continued to fuss over me until I fell asleep in the arm-chair after a meal of hot *eba* and *egusı* soup.

I had a very bad dream in which my skull was being crushed by a trailer. I also know for sure that I did not get the job for the interview of which set the pace for the just recounted tale.

The Daughter

I eventually got a job. But it wasn't the kind of job I had hoped for. An aunt of mine had set up a day-care centre and invited me to come and handle the kids — the fairly older ones.

The pay was not too good but still, it was better than nothing. At least when I woke up every morning, I knew I was going somewhere.

I handled the class of six to seven year olds, and mind you, they were about thirty in number. I taught them spellings, addition, poetry or rhymes, as it was called. I also took them on games and excursion trips.

I remember in my first class with them, I had asked them all for their names but none was significant enough to strike any cord in my mind at that time. By the fourth week, I knew each of them by their first names at least, and somehow I had began to enjoy my job.

Childhood innocence has a soothing effect on the nerves in a way that is somewhat psychologically inexplicable. In this rat race which we call human existence, a four hour, five day a week contact with children was a sufficient soul purgation; a catharsis of sorts for me. It in a lot of ways made up for the inadequate pay and my aunty's proud and vain gait. I couldn't ask for more.

But I got more one particular day when this little girl was left with me after all the others had gone home.

"Grandma said she is going to be late in coming to pick me today," she said in her tiny voice.

"Why," I asked.

"She has a meeting," she answered. Her name was Anita, a very bright girl with lovely eyes and a long mane of hair.

"It's okay," I said to her. "You can stay here with me until she comes."

I usually stayed in the office until at least 5.pm. I didn't believe anyone ought to close from work before five.

"I like you, Uncle," Anita said. "You look like my Daddy."

"Where does your Daddy work?"

"New York. The United Nations Peace Movement."

"What's his name?"

"Dr. Anthony Akingbe."

"Your mother, what's her name, what does she do?"

"Her name was Anita, and she died when I was a little girl."

"In a car accident?" I didn't want to ask to hurt her, but I had to be sure.

"Yes," she answered. I saw the lump form in her threat.

I didn't know how it happened but the little girl was in my arms and we were both sobbing. Many thoughts ran through my brain but the most prominent was what a small place this world is. Her voice stopped my thoughts.

"You knew my mummy?"

I though a while before I answered. "In a way," I said.

"Daddy told me she was a very nice woman. Is it true?"

"Yes," I answered.

"That she always wanted the world to be a better place."

"Yes." I swallowed.

"Then we should stop crying. You and I, we can make the world a better place, can't we?" She looked into my face with a genuine need for an answer.

"Yes." I smiled.

And then she smiled too. And somehow I knew it was going to be alright.

****

With that, I end my tales. Friend, it is my hope that I have not bored you with my experiences and encounters when only such wandering allowed me to maintain my sanity.

It is also my hope that you have, in the course of these stories, learnt a thing or two. If this is true then I would rest, knowing that this whole exercise hasn't been a completely futile one. As such, I would therefore urge you to keep such learnt lessons close to your heart as they may become useful in some not too distant future. Till the time comes for some other tales to be told, I bid you farewell friend. Thanks for sparing the time.

www.ingramcontent.com/pod-product-compliance
Lightning Source LLC
LaVergne TN
LVHW041546070526
838199LV00046B/1850